COLOR CUT CREATE

PAPER TOY
DINOSAUR
WORLD

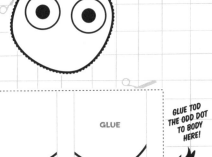

GLUE

GLUE

GLUE TOD
THE ODD DOT
TO BODY
HERE!

CREATED BY MERRILL RAINEY
ODD DOT • NEW YORK

ALLOSAURUS

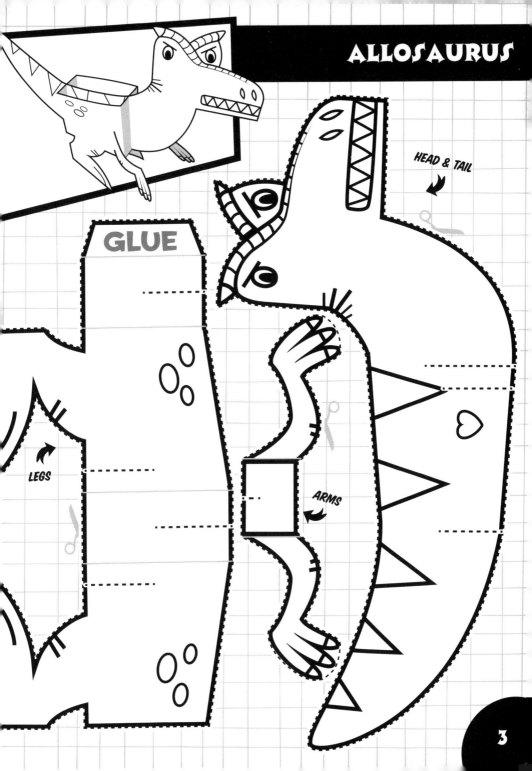

HEAD & TAIL

GLUE

LEGS

ARMS

3

4

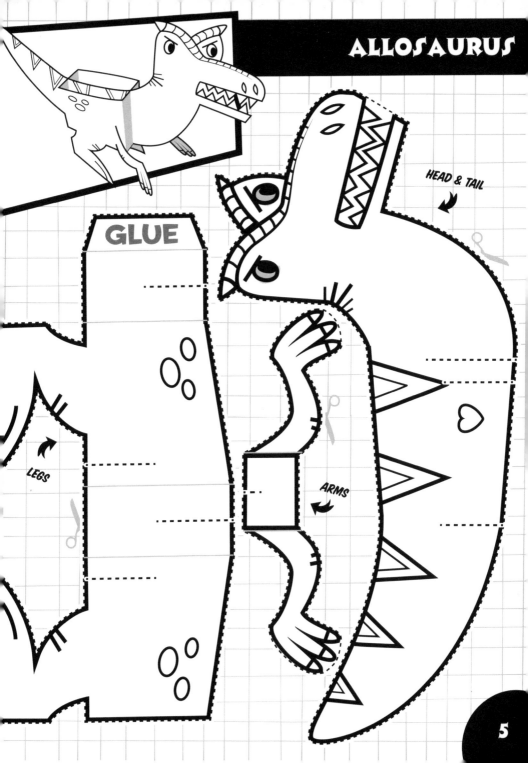

ALLOSAURUS

HEAD & TAIL

GLUE

LEGS

ARMS

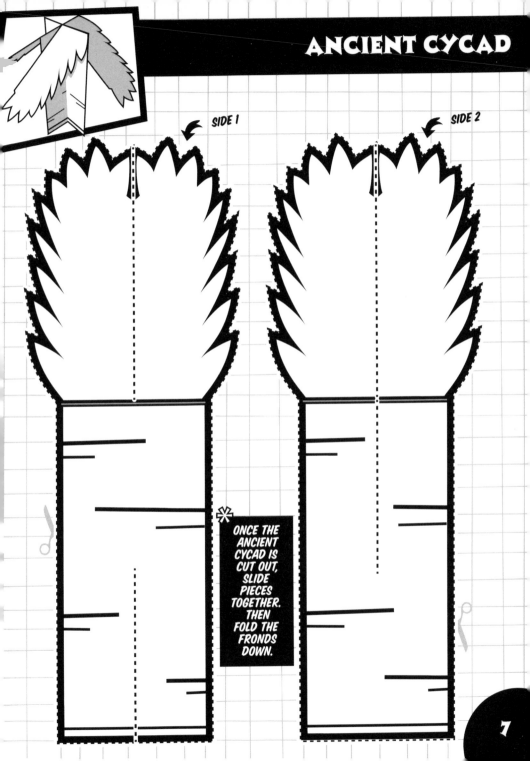

ANCIENT CYCAD

SIDE 1

SIDE 2

* ONCE THE ANCIENT CYCAD IS CUT OUT, SLIDE PIECES TOGETHER. THEN FOLD THE FRONDS DOWN.

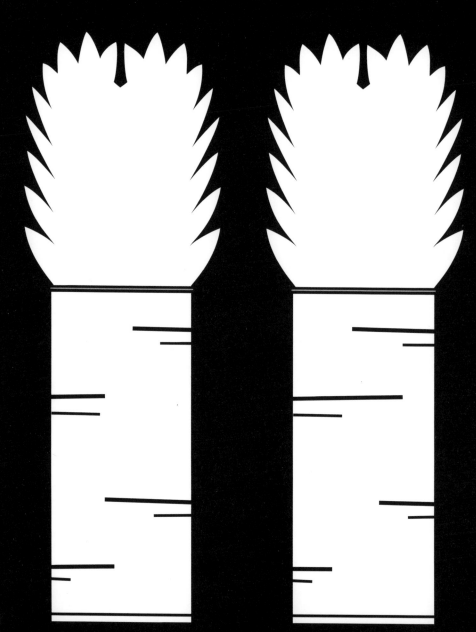

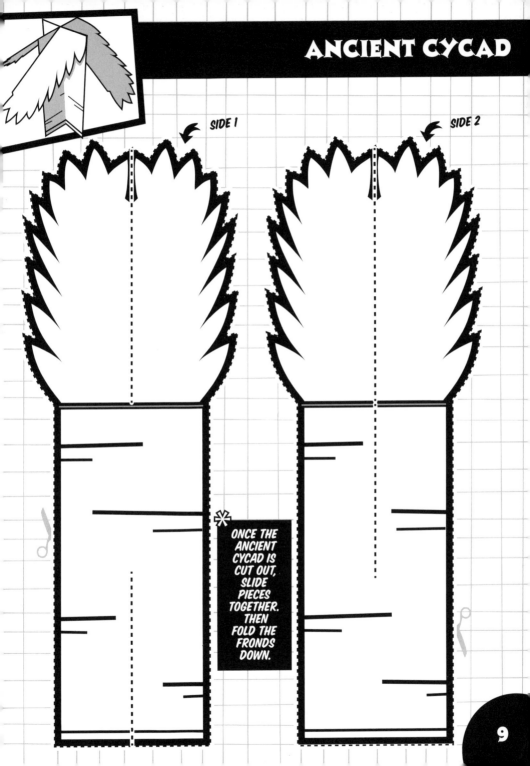

SIDE 1

SIDE 2

* ONCE THE ANCIENT CYCAD IS CUT OUT, SLIDE PIECES TOGETHER. THEN FOLD THE FRONDS DOWN.

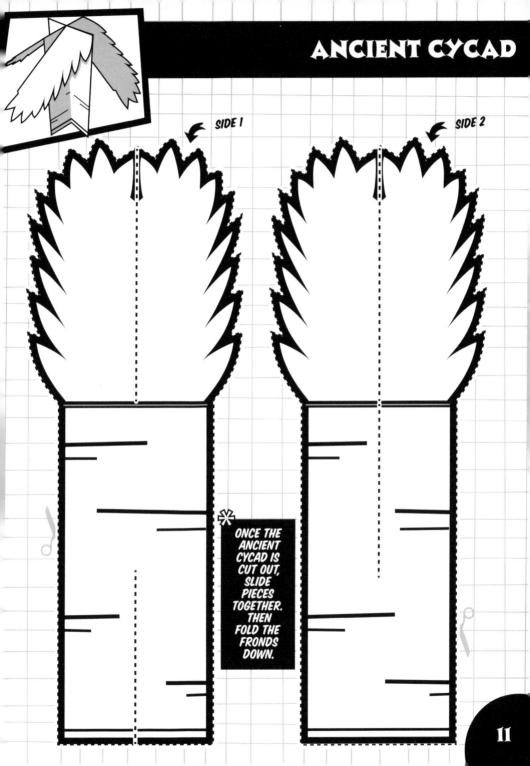

ANCIENT CYCAD

SIDE 1

SIDE 2

※ ONCE THE ANCIENT CYCAD IS CUT OUT, SLIDE PIECES TOGETHER. THEN FOLD THE FRONDS DOWN.

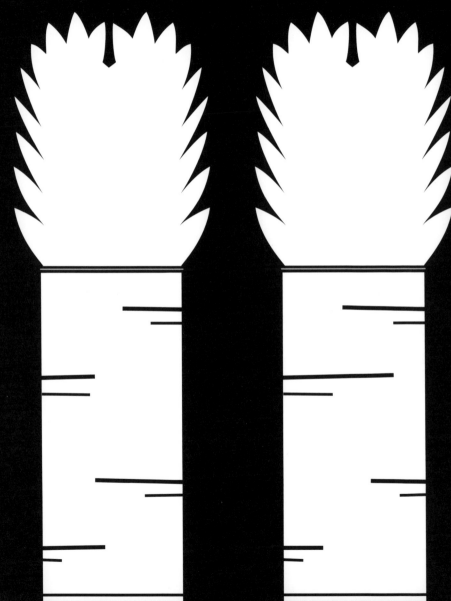

ROCK
(SIDE 1)

GLUE

SHELL

ROCK
(SIDE 2)

GLUE
SHELL TO TOP
OF BODY

HEAD, LEGS & TAIL

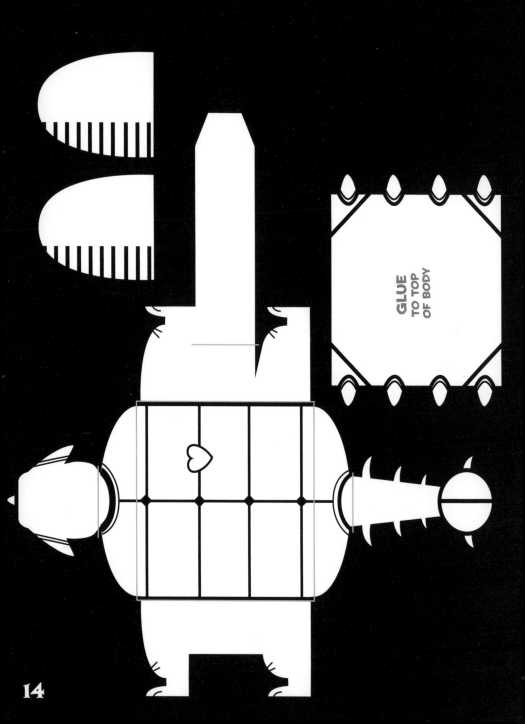

GLUE
TO TOP
OF BODY

14

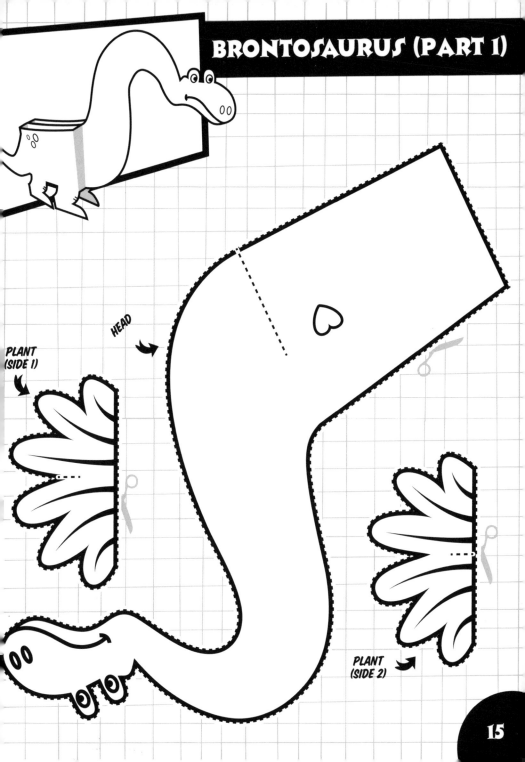

BRONTOSAURUS (PART 1)

PLANT
(SIDE 1)

HEAD

PLANT
(SIDE 2)

15

LEGS

GLUE
HEAD & TAIL
PIECES TOGETHER

TAIL

GLUE

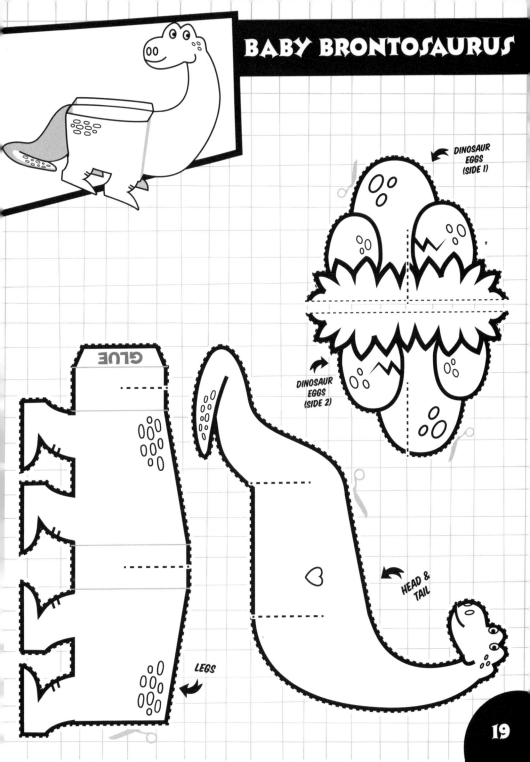

BABY BRONTOSAURUS

DINOSAUR EGGS (SIDE 1)

DINOSAUR EGGS (SIDE 2)

GLUE

HEAD & TAIL

LEGS

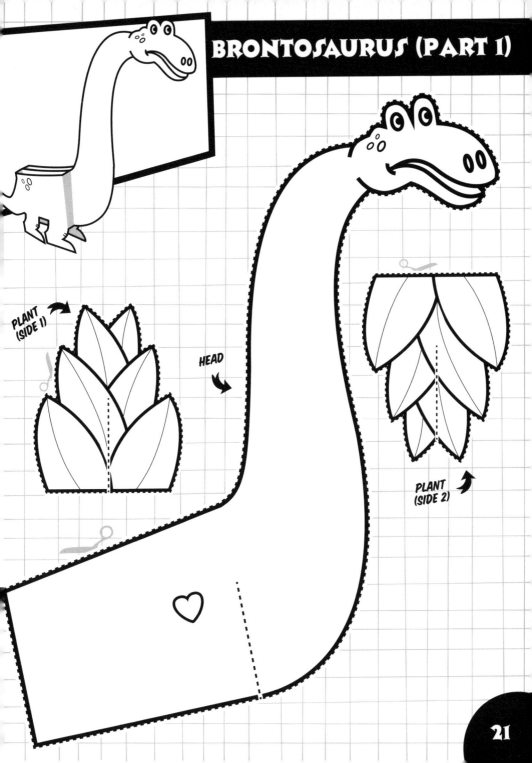

PLANT
(SIDE 1)

HEAD

PLANT
(SIDE 2)

LEGS

GLUE
HEAD & TAIL
PIECES TOGETHER

TAIL

GLUE

BOULDERS

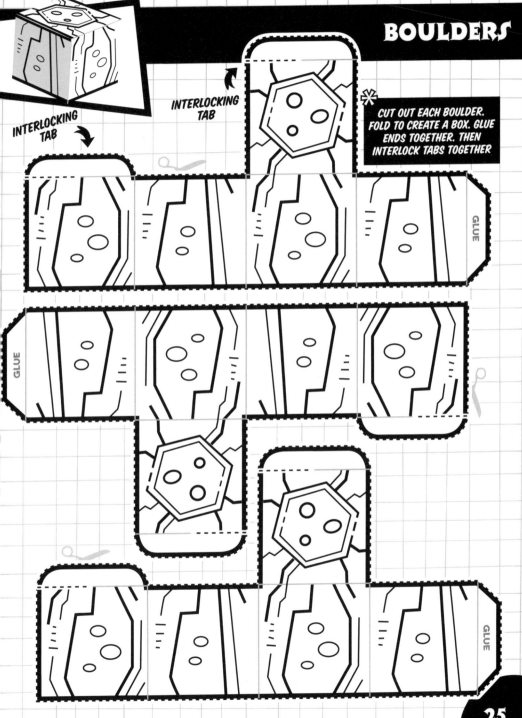

INTERLOCKING TAB

INTERLOCKING TAB

CUT OUT EACH BOULDER. FOLD TO CREATE A BOX. GLUE ENDS TOGETHER. THEN INTERLOCK TABS TOGETHER

GLUE

GLUE

GLUE

25

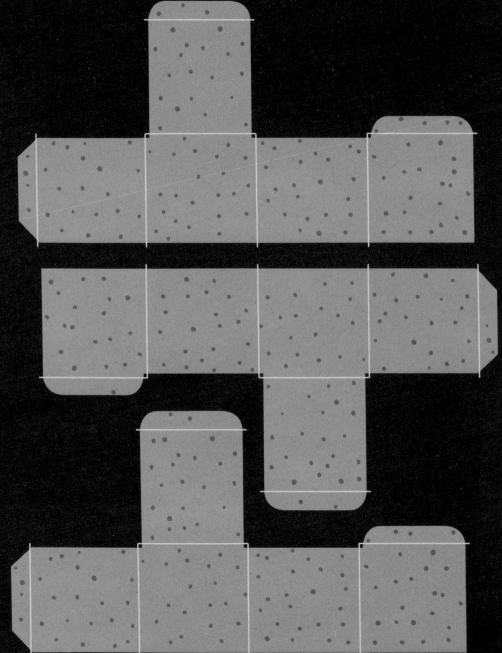

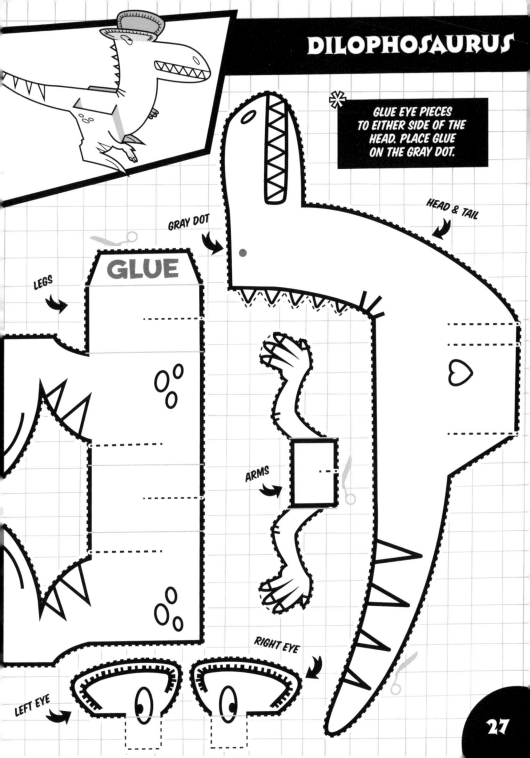

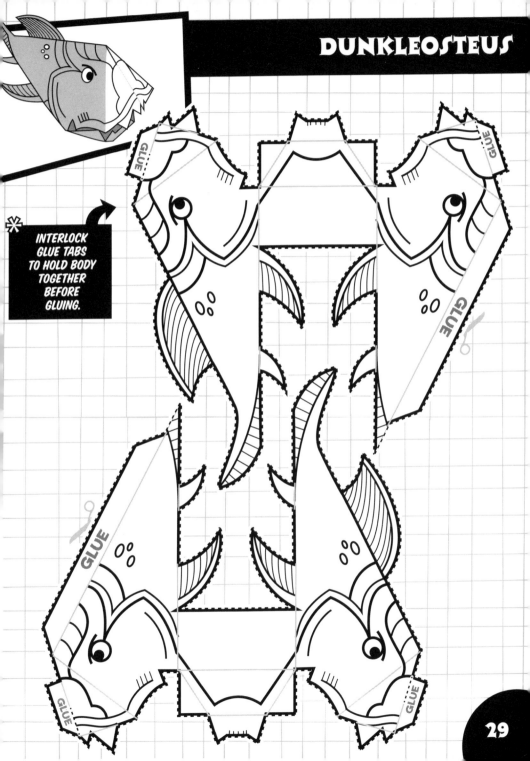

DUNKLEOSTEUS

✱ INTERLOCK GLUE TABS TO HOLD BODY TOGETHER BEFORE GLUING.

GLUE

GLUE

GLUE

GLUE

GLUE

GLUE

29

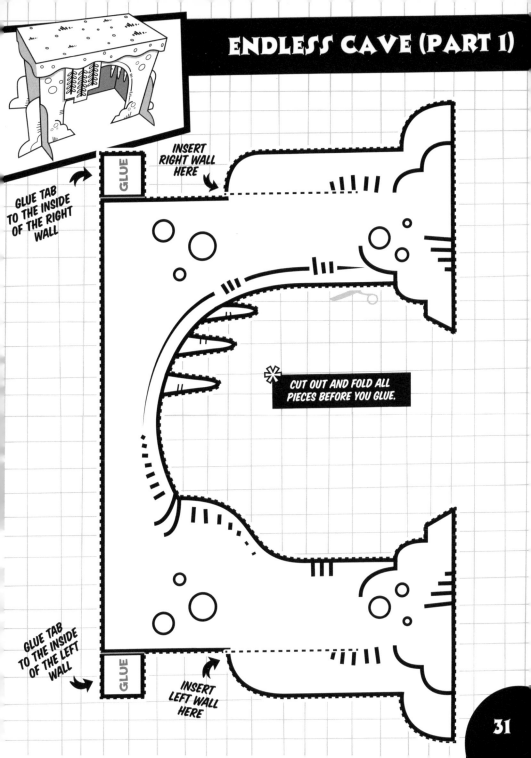

GLUE TAB TO THE INSIDE OF THE RIGHT WALL

GLUE

INSERT RIGHT WALL HERE

✳ CUT OUT AND FOLD ALL PIECES BEFORE YOU GLUE.

GLUE TAB TO THE INSIDE OF THE LEFT WALL

GLUE

INSERT LEFT WALL HERE

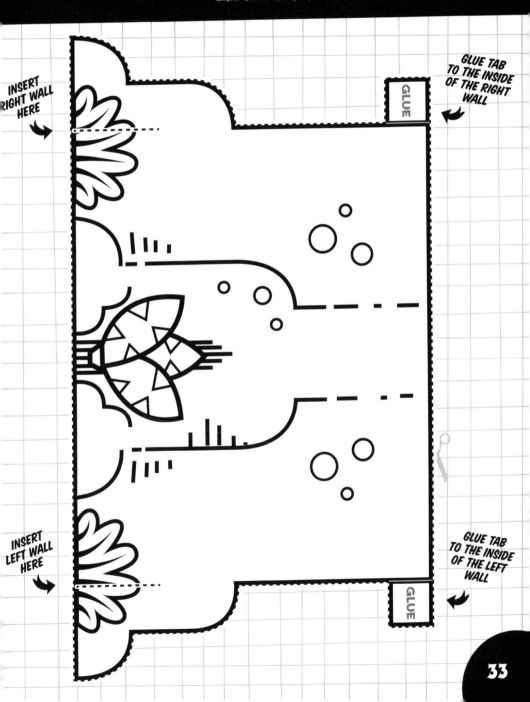

INSERT RIGHT WALL HERE

GLUE TAB TO THE INSIDE OF THE RIGHT WALL

GLUE

INSERT LEFT WALL HERE

GLUE TAB TO THE INSIDE OF THE LEFT WALL

GLUE

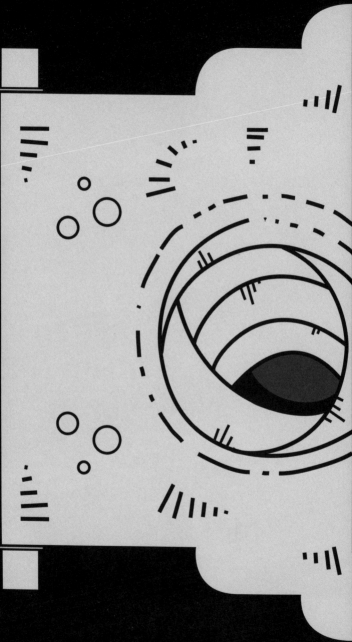

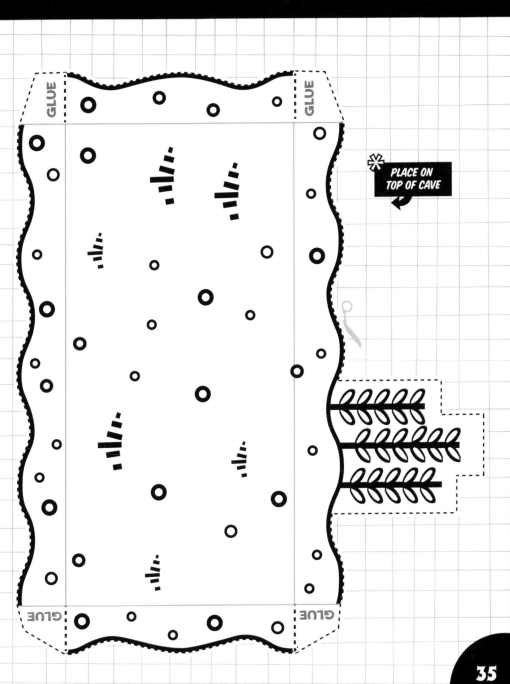

GLUE

GLUE

✳ PLACE ON TOP OF CAVE

GLUE

GLUE

35

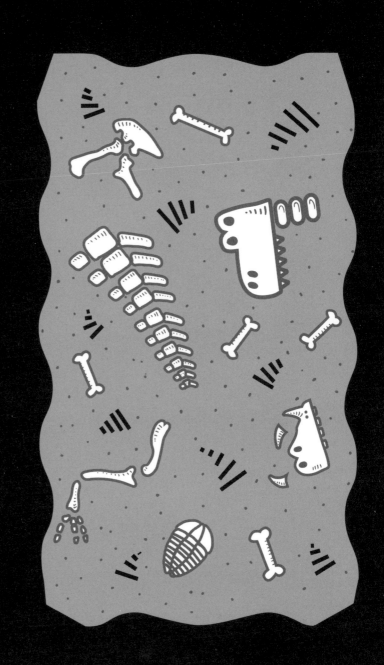

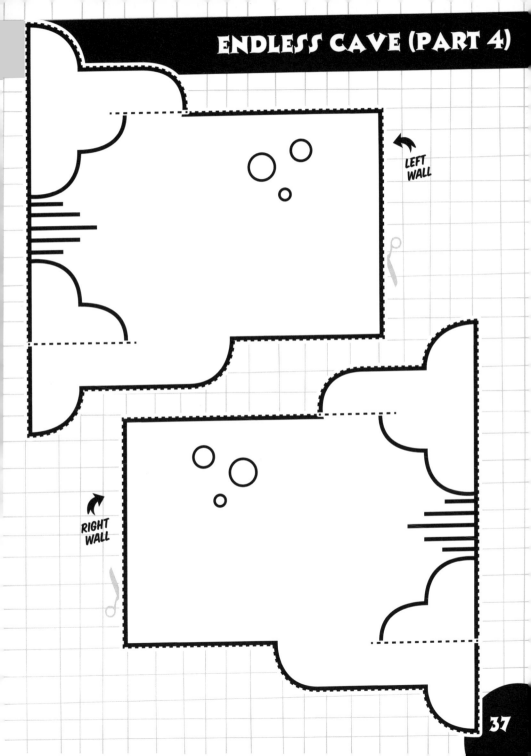

LEFT
WALL

RIGHT
WALL

44

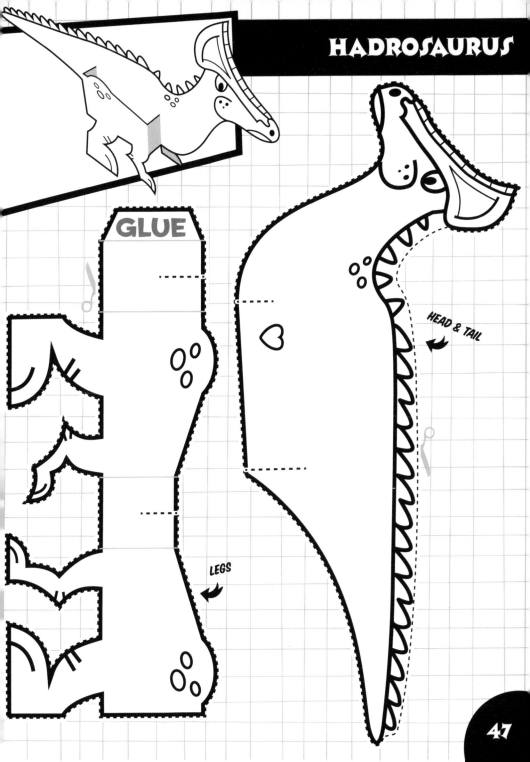

HADROSAURUS

GLUE

HEAD & TAIL

LEGS

47

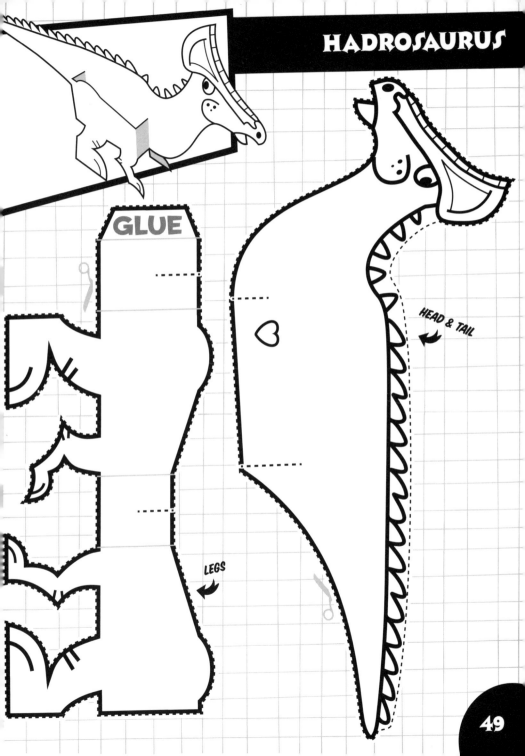

HADROSAURUS

GLUE

HEAD & TAIL

LEGS

49

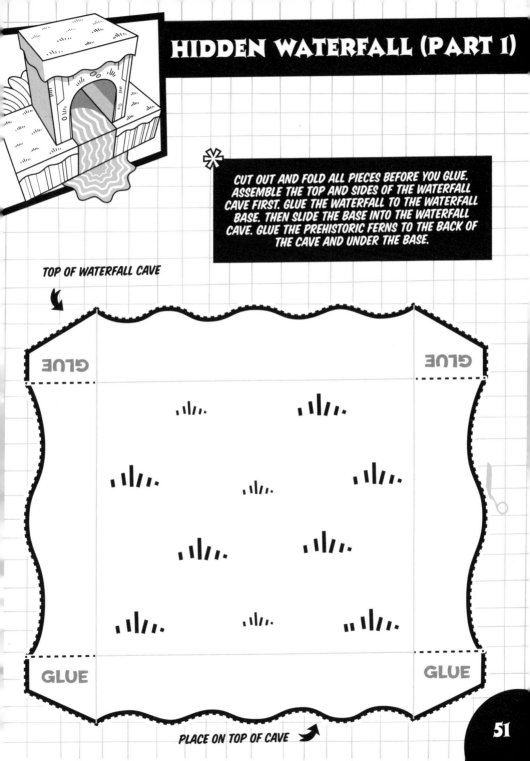

HIDDEN WATERFALL (PART 1)

CUT OUT AND FOLD ALL PIECES BEFORE YOU GLUE.
ASSEMBLE THE TOP AND SIDES OF THE WATERFALL
CAVE FIRST. GLUE THE WATERFALL TO THE WATERFALL
BASE. THEN SLIDE THE BASE INTO THE WATERFALL
CAVE. GLUE THE PREHISTORIC FERNS TO THE BACK OF
THE CAVE AND UNDER THE BASE.

TOP OF WATERFALL CAVE

GLUE

GLUE

GLUE

GLUE

PLACE ON TOP OF CAVE

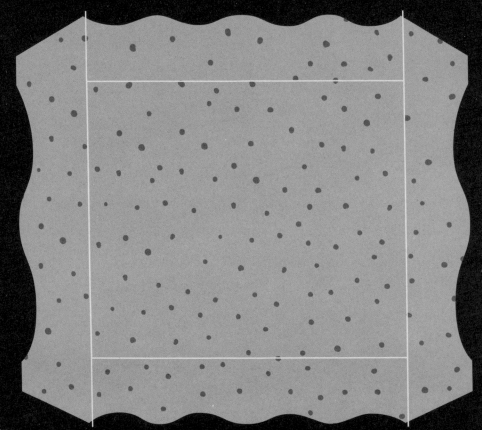

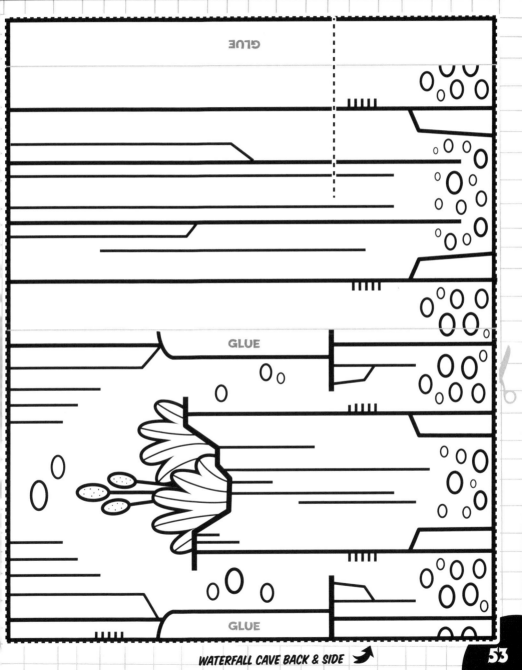

GLUE

GLUE

GLUE

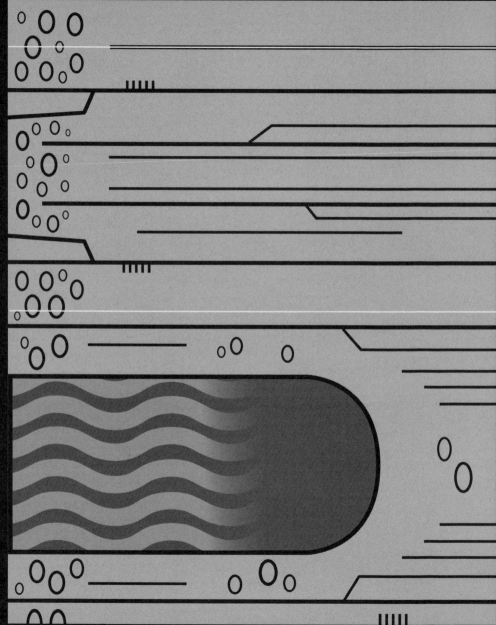

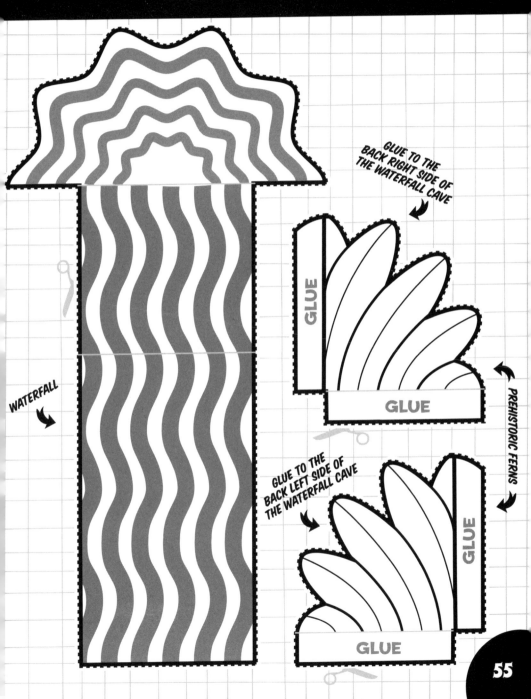

GLUE TO THE BACK RIGHT SIDE OF THE WATERFALL CAVE

GLUE

GLUE

PREHISTORIC FERNS

WATERFALL

GLUE TO THE BACK LEFT SIDE OF THE WATERFALL CAVE

GLUE

GLUE

GLUE

GLUE

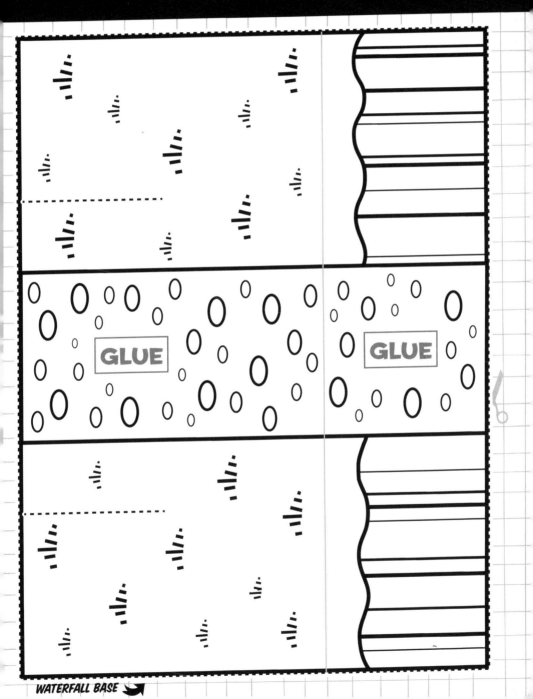

GLUE

GLUE

WATERFALL BASE

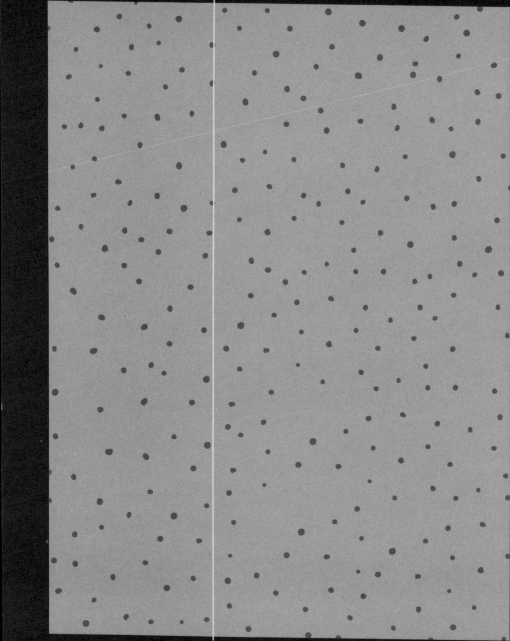

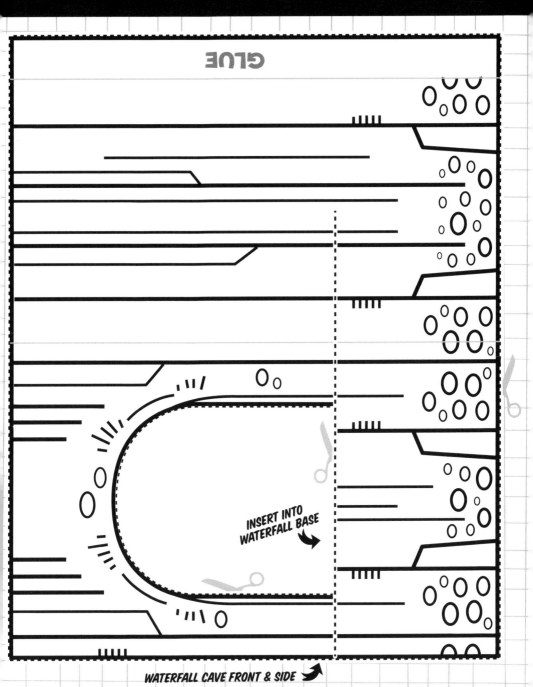

GLUE

INSERT INTO
WATERFALL BASE

WATERFALL CAVE FRONT & SIDE

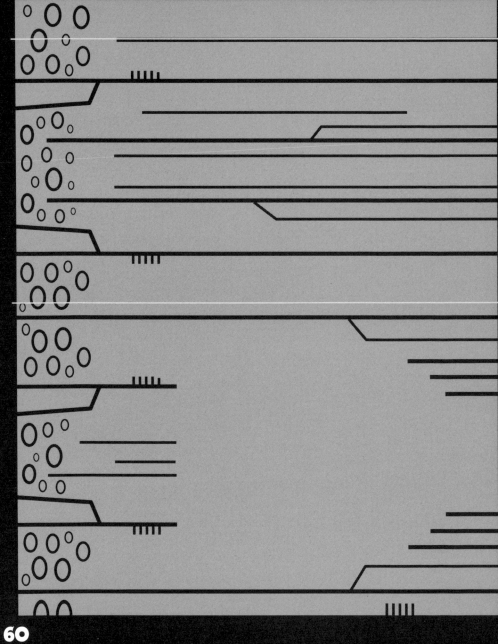

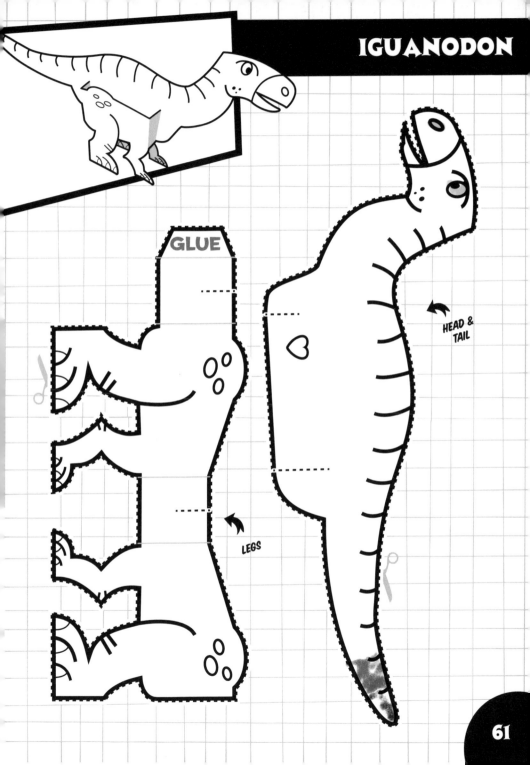

IGUANODON

GLUE

HEAD & TAIL

LEGS

61

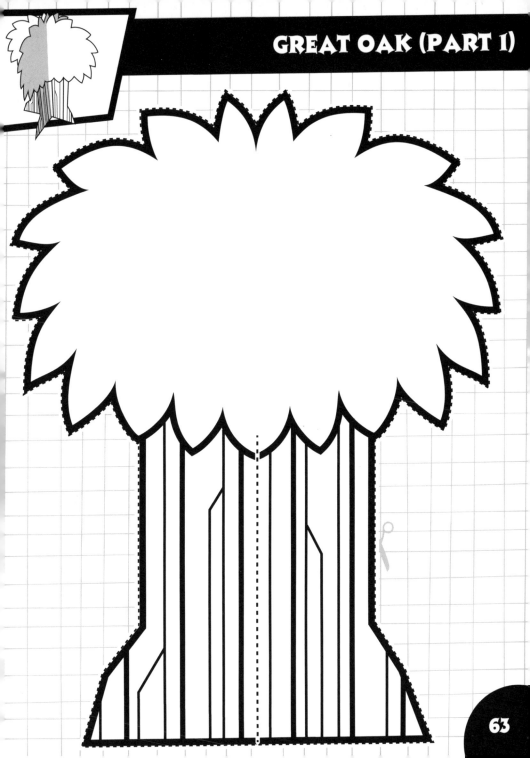

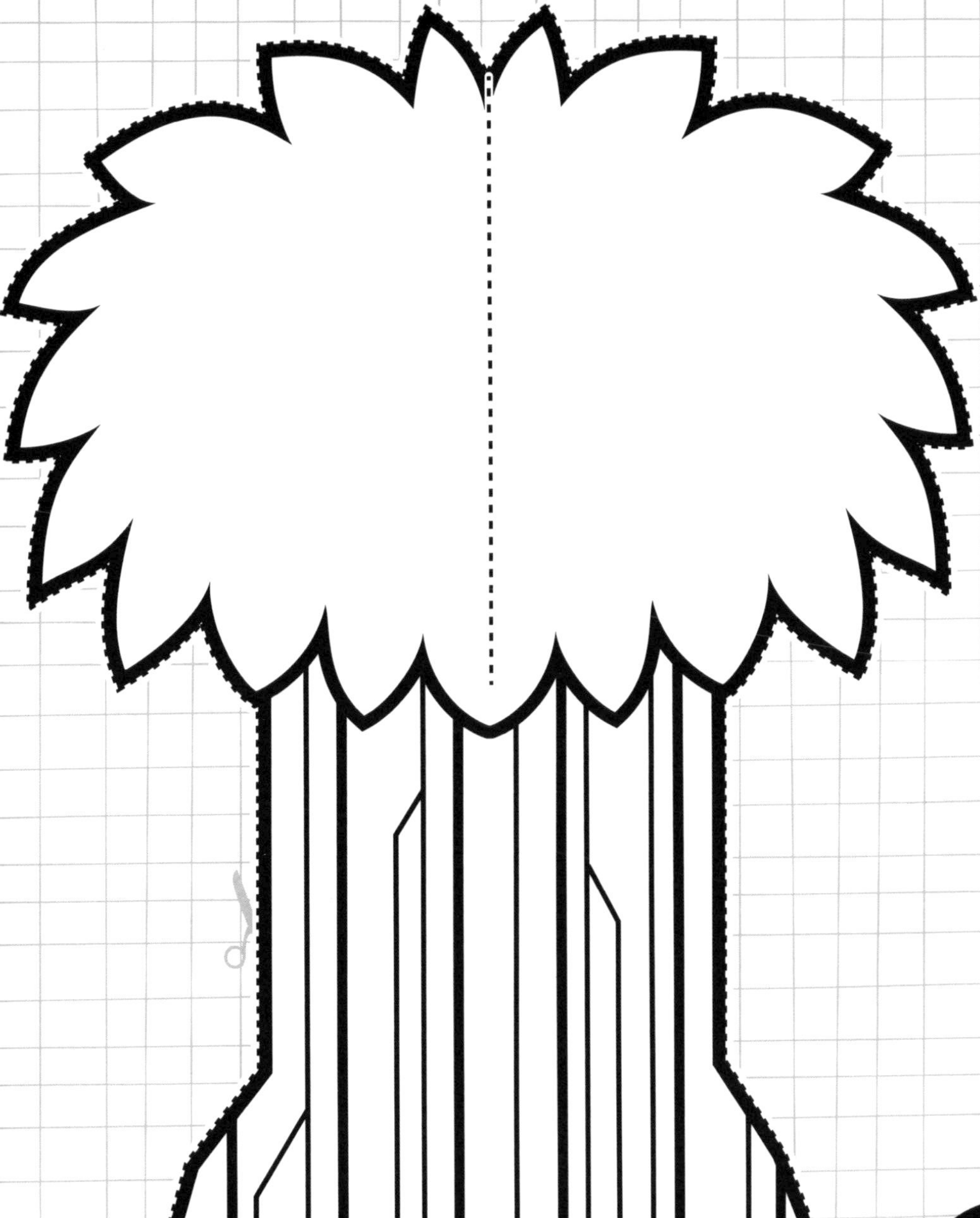

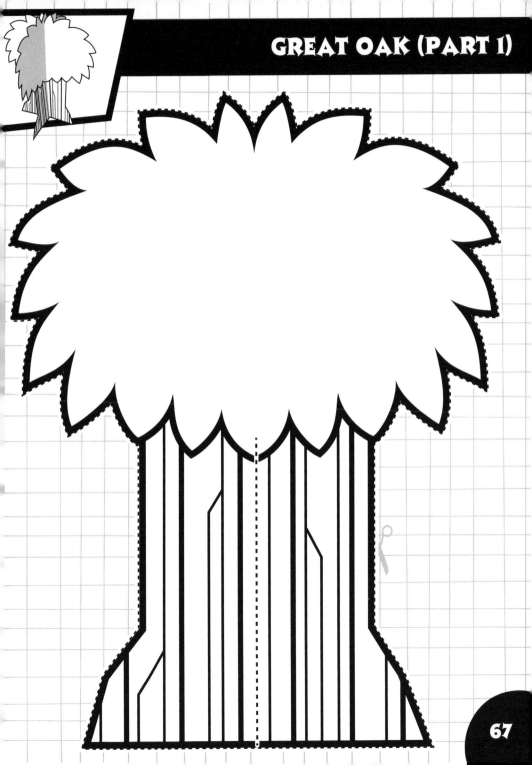

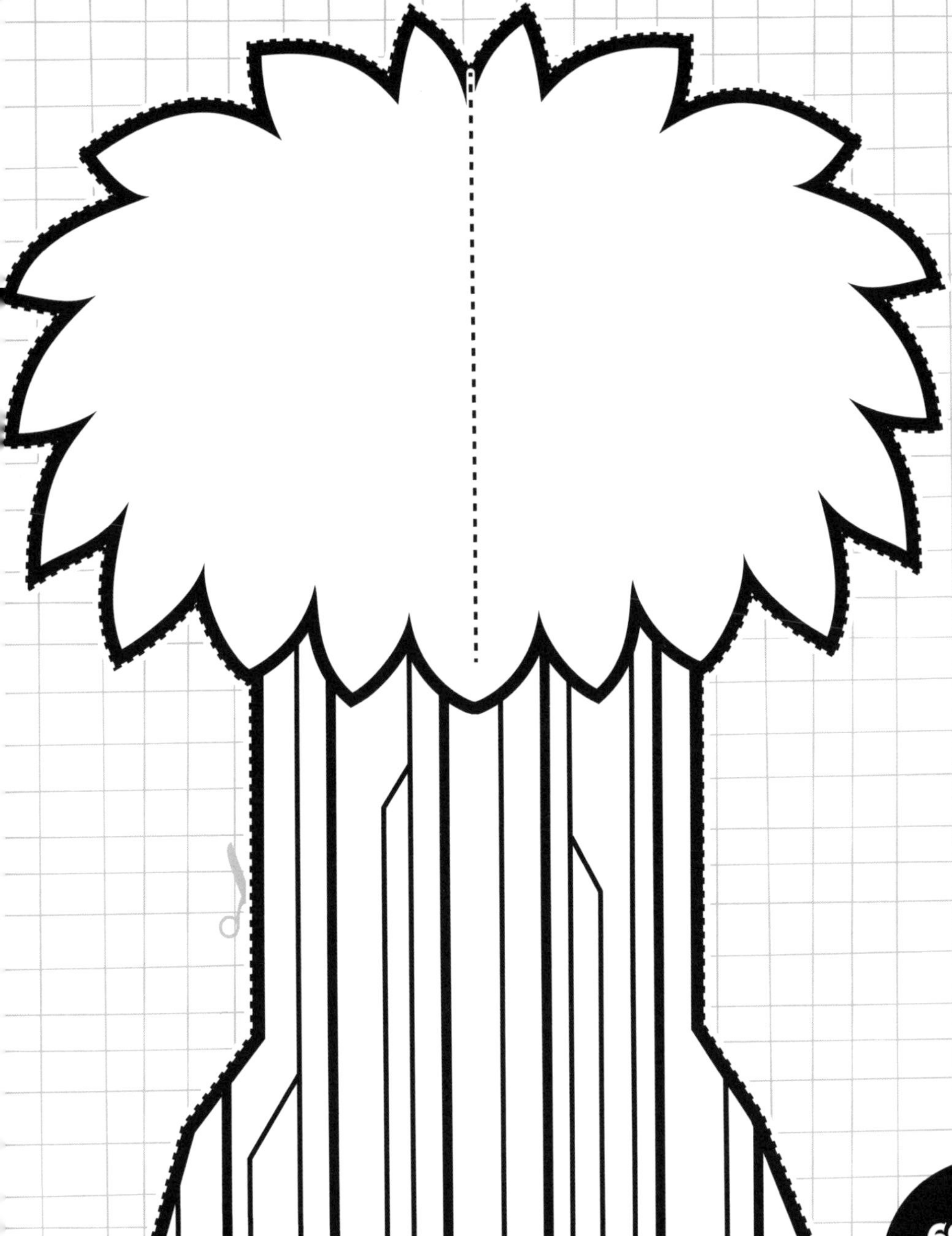

70

GLUE

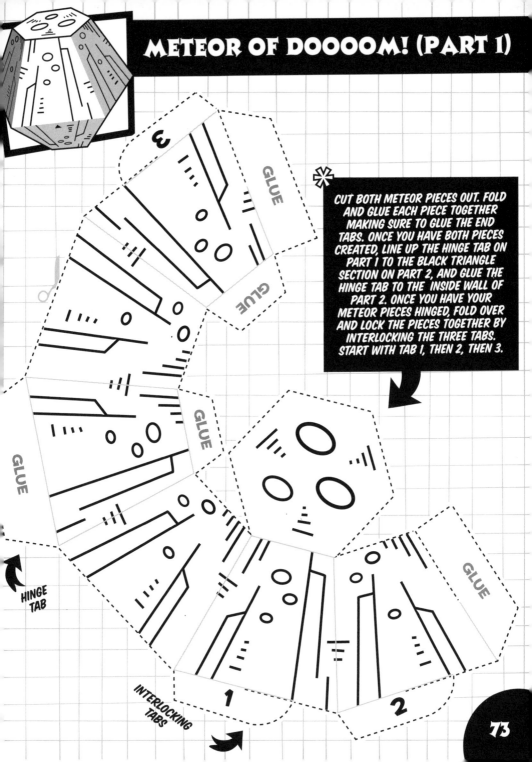

CUT BOTH METEOR PIECES OUT. FOLD AND GLUE EACH PIECE TOGETHER MAKING SURE TO GLUE THE END TABS. ONCE YOU HAVE BOTH PIECES CREATED, LINE UP THE HINGE TAB ON PART 1 TO THE BLACK TRIANGLE SECTION ON PART 2, AND GLUE THE HINGE TAB TO THE INSIDE WALL OF PART 2. ONCE YOU HAVE YOUR METEOR PIECES HINGED, FOLD OVER AND LOCK THE PIECES TOGETHER BY INTERLOCKING THE THREE TABS. START WITH TAB 1, THEN 2, THEN 3.

GLUE

GLUE

GLUE

GLUE

GLUE

GLUE

HINGE TAB

INTERLOCKING TABS

3

1

2

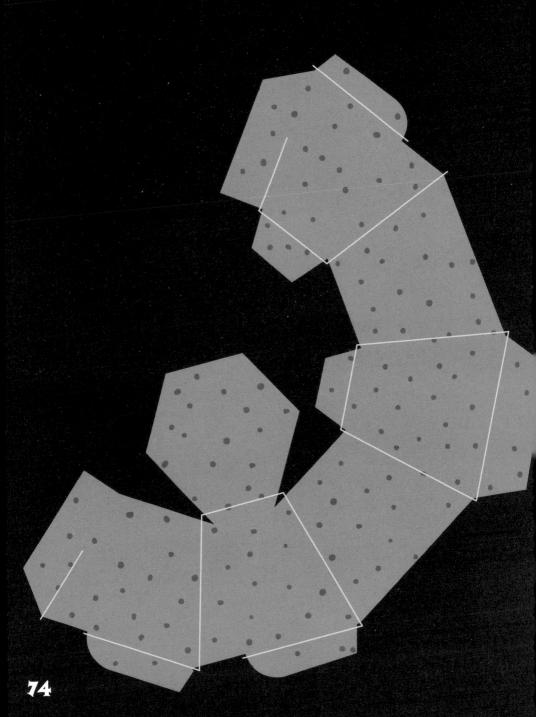

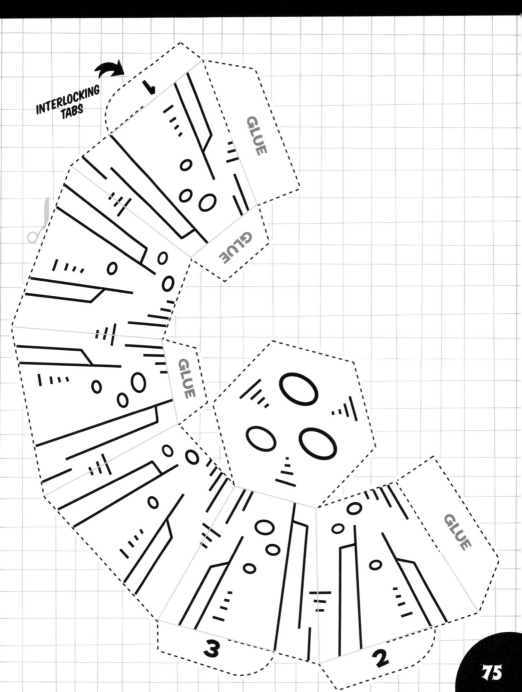

INTERLOCKING TABS

GLUE

GLUE

GLUE

GLUE

3

2

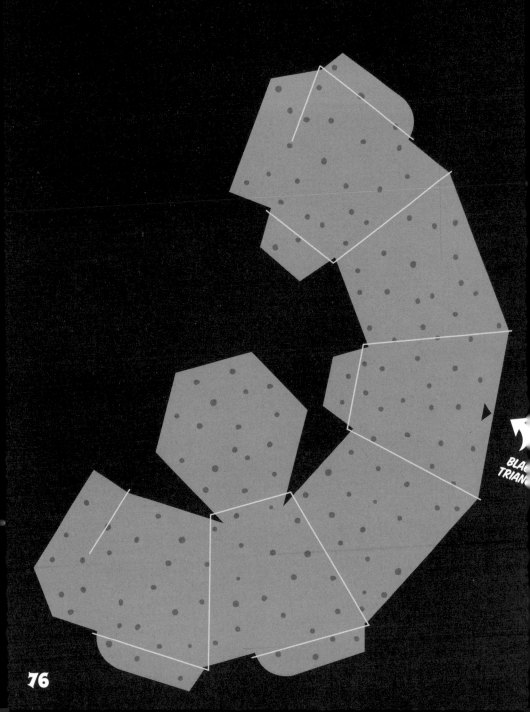

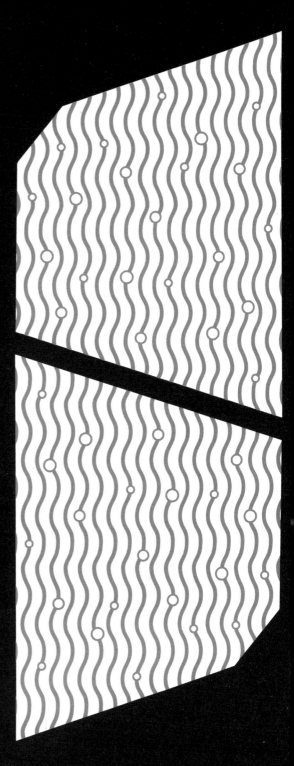

GLUE

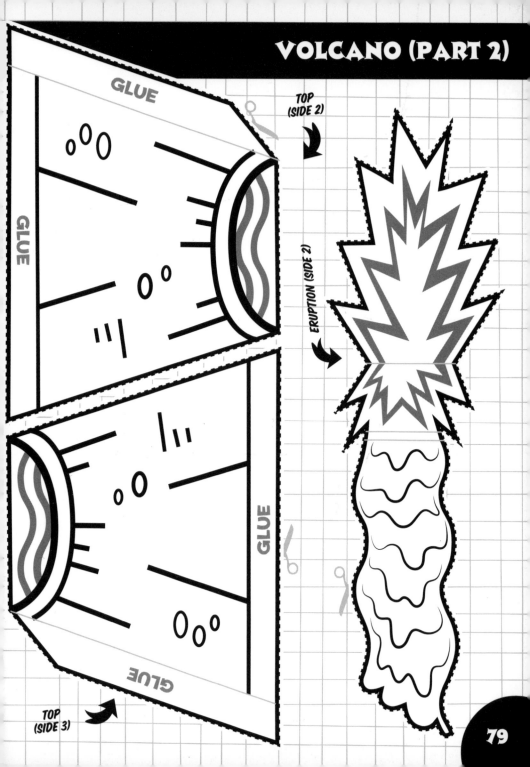

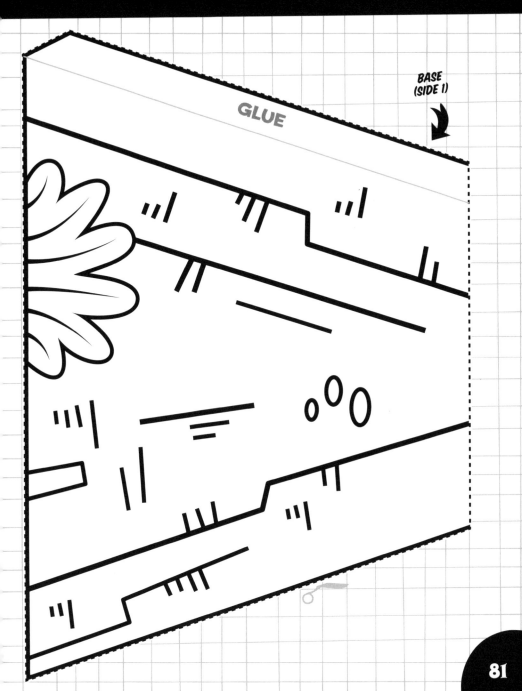

GLUE

BASE
(SIDE 1)

GLUE

BASE
(SIDE 2)

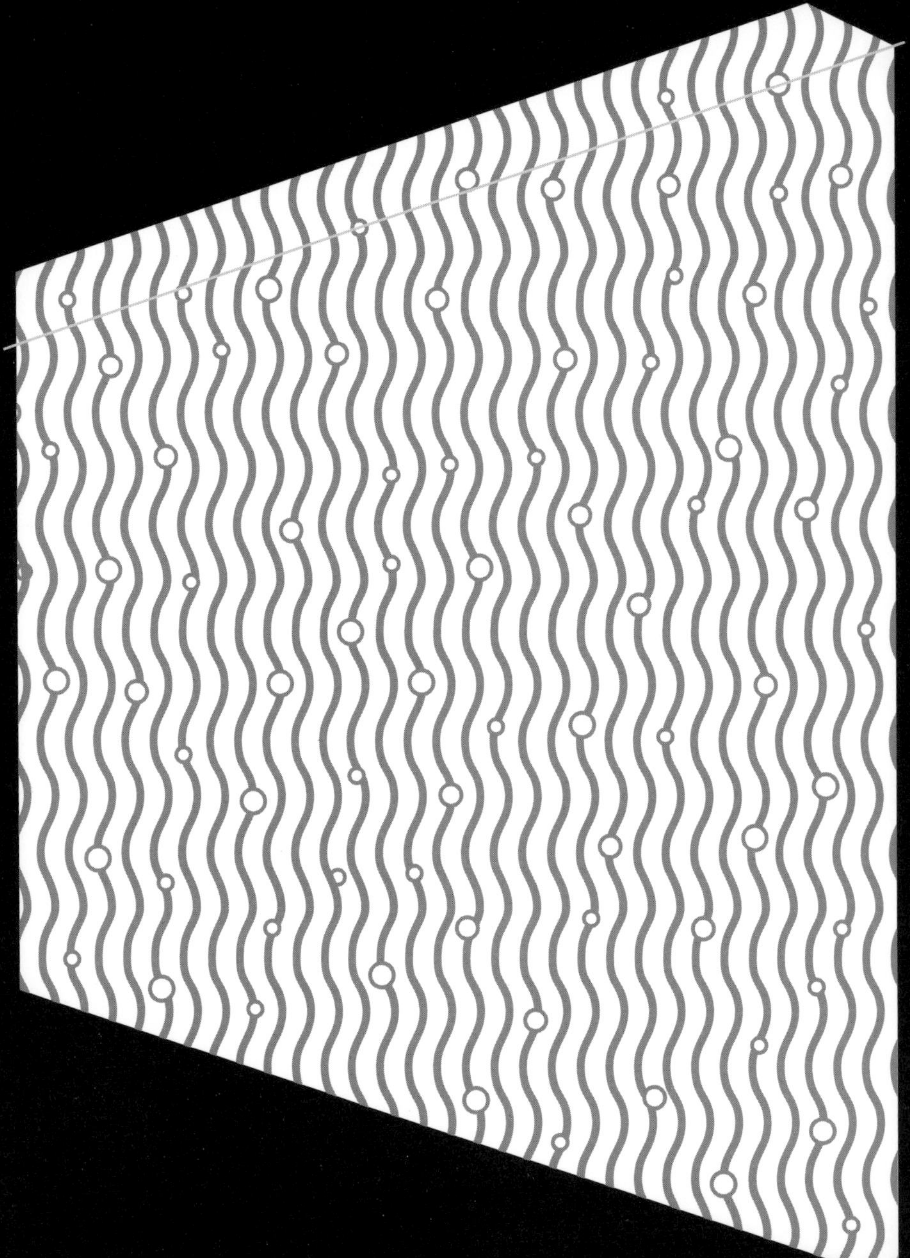

GLUE

BASE
(SIDE 3)

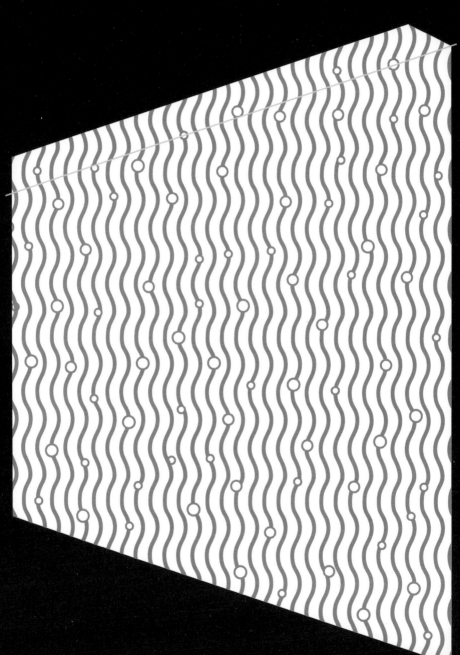

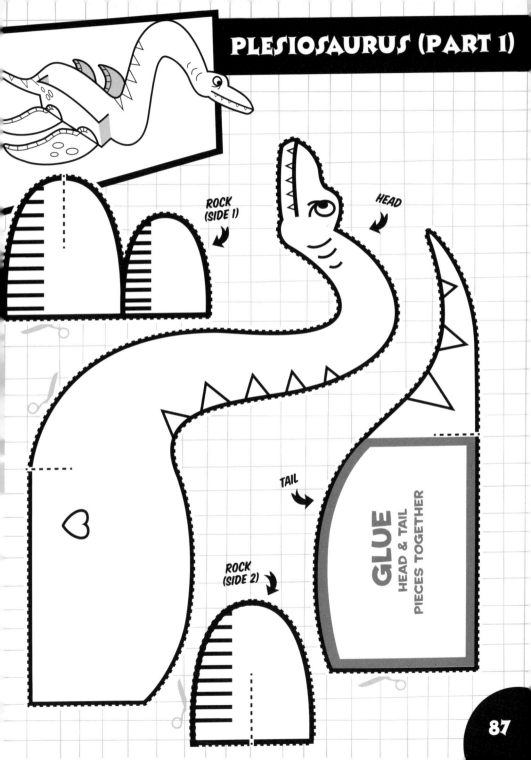

PLESIOSAURUS (PART 1)

ROCK (SIDE 1)

HEAD

TAIL

ROCK (SIDE 2)

GLUE
HEAD & TAIL
PIECES TOGETHER

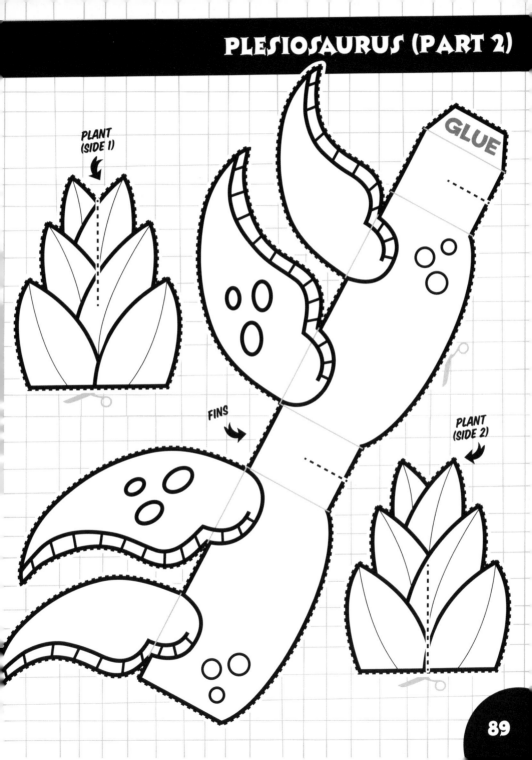

PLANT
(SIDE 1)

GLUE

FINS

PLANT
(SIDE 2)

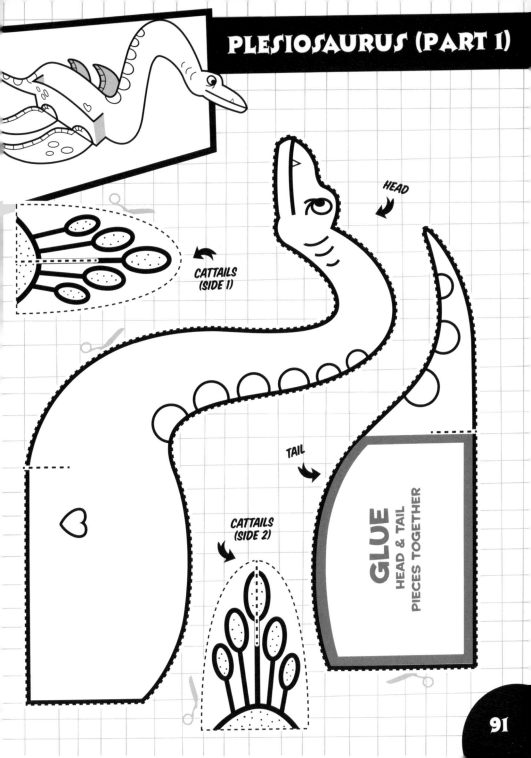

CATTAILS
(SIDE 1)

HEAD

TAIL

CATTAILS
(SIDE 2)

GLUE
HEAD & TAIL
PIECES TOGETHER

PLESIOSAURUS (PART 2)

GLUE THE SEAWEED PIECES TOGETHER. THEN FOLD ON THE GRAY LINES.

GLUE

THORNY SEAWEED (SIDE 1)

FINS

THORNY SEAWEED (SIDE 2)

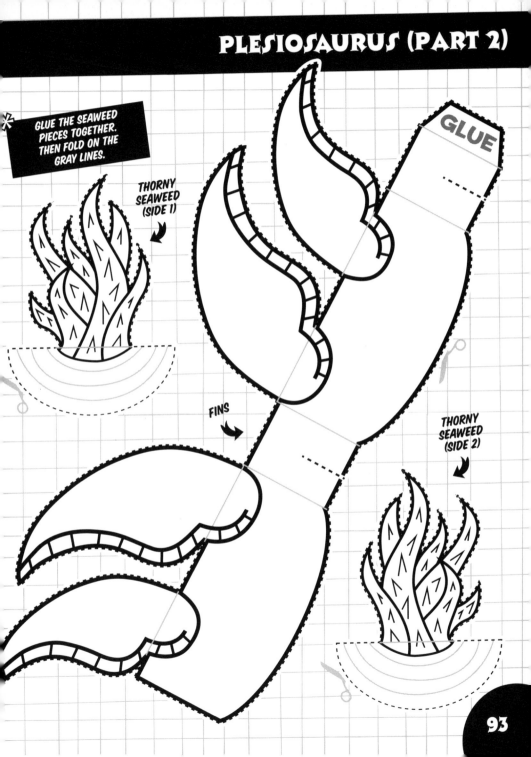

PROTOCERATOPS

INSERT FRILL

LEGS

HEAD & TAIL

FRILL

GLUE

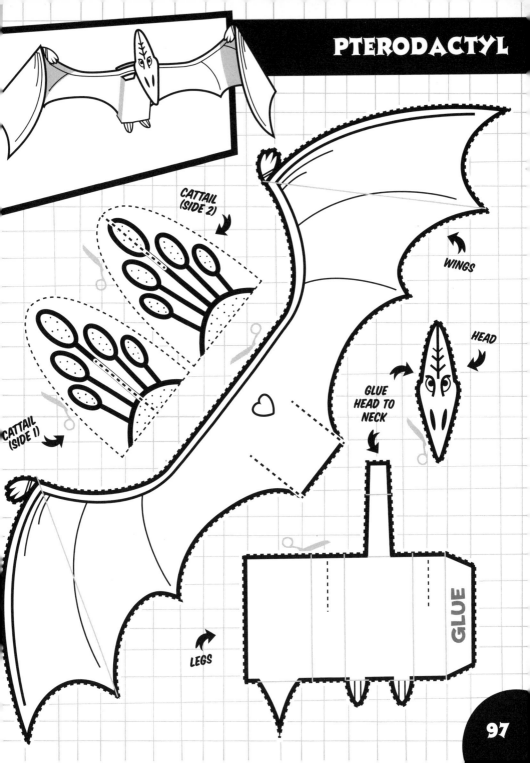

PTERODACTYL

CATTAIL (SIDE 2)

WINGS

HEAD

GLUE HEAD TO NECK

CATTAIL (SIDE 1)

GLUE

LEGS

97

GLUE

PTERODACTYL

PLANT
(SIDE 1)

PLANT
(SIDE 2)

WINGS

LEGS

GLUE

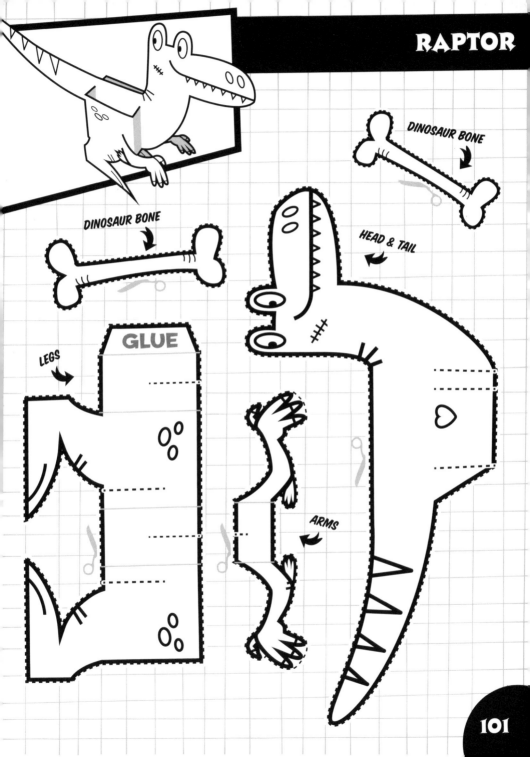

RAPTOR

DINOSAUR BONE

DINOSAUR BONE

HEAD & TAIL

GLUE

LEGS

ARMS

101

102

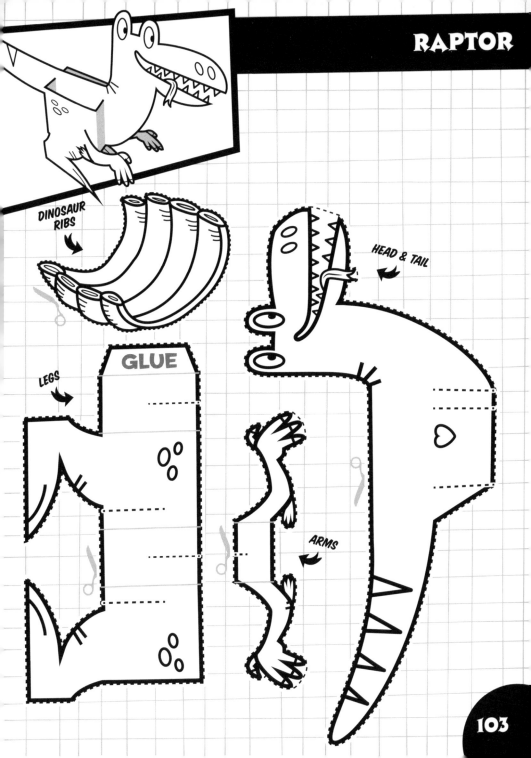

RAPTOR

DINOSAUR RIBS

HEAD & TAIL

LEGS

GLUE

ARMS

103

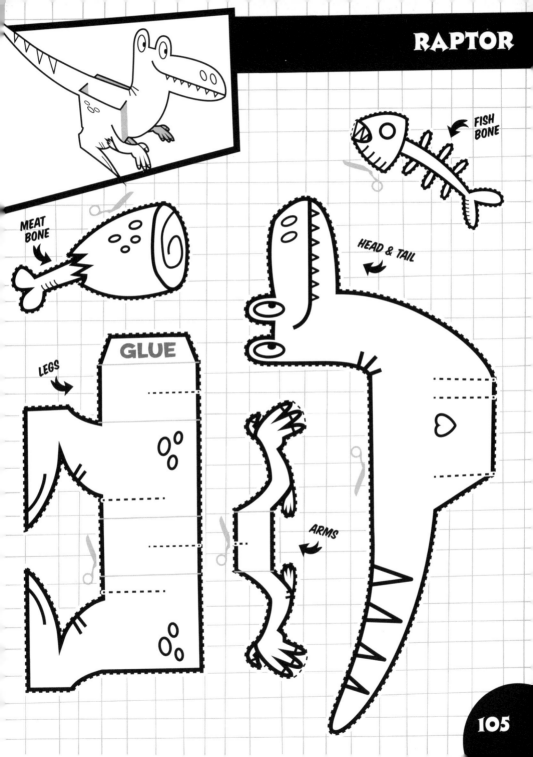

RAPTOR

FISH BONE

MEAT BONE

HEAD & TAIL

GLUE

LEGS

ARMS

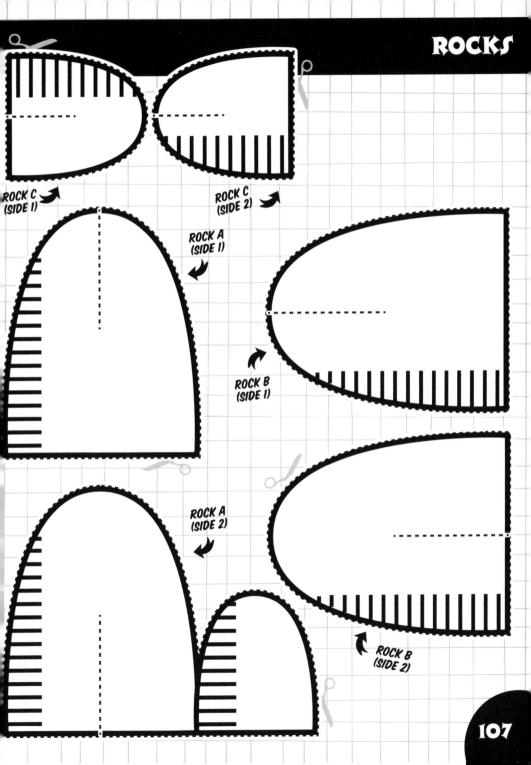

ROCKS

ROCK C
(SIDE 1)

ROCK C
(SIDE 2)

ROCK A
(SIDE 1)

ROCK B
(SIDE 1)

ROCK A
(SIDE 2)

ROCK B
(SIDE 2)

108

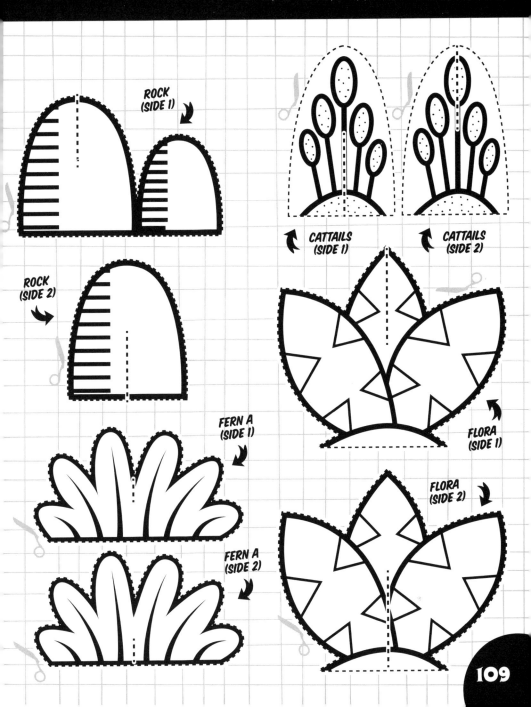

ROCK (SIDE 1)

CATTAILS (SIDE 1)

CATTAILS (SIDE 2)

ROCK (SIDE 2)

FERN A (SIDE 1)

FLORA (SIDE 1)

FERN A (SIDE 2)

FLORA (SIDE 2)

109

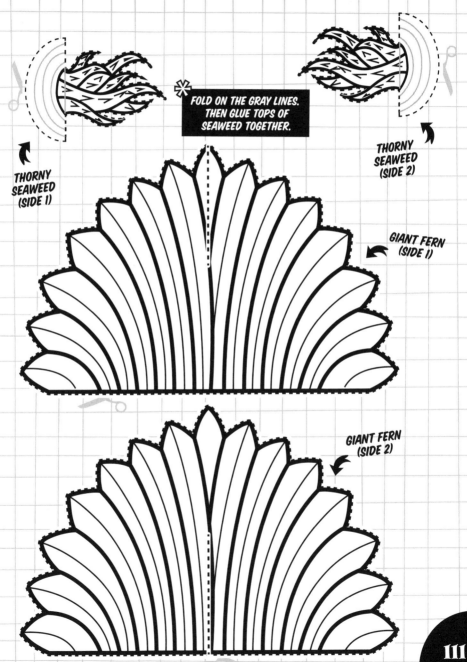

FOLD ON THE GRAY LINES.
THEN GLUE TOPS OF
SEAWEED TOGETHER.

THORNY
SEAWEED
(SIDE 1)

THORNY
SEAWEED
(SIDE 2)

GIANT FERN
(SIDE 1)

GIANT FERN
(SIDE 2)

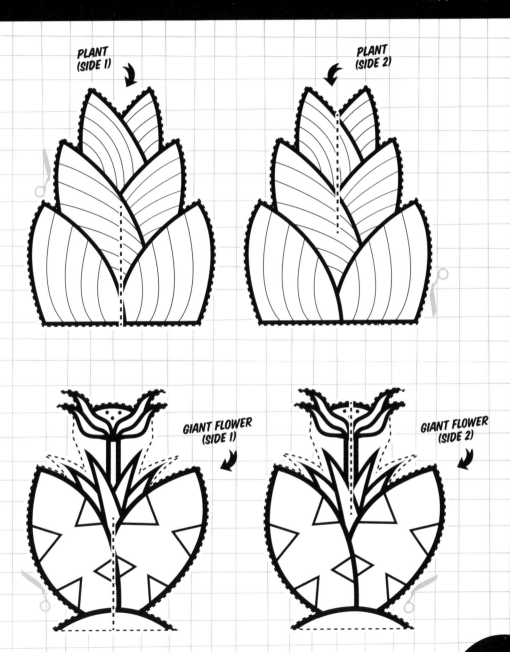

PLANT
(SIDE 1)

PLANT
(SIDE 2)

GIANT FLOWER
(SIDE 1)

GIANT FLOWER
(SIDE 2)

113

114

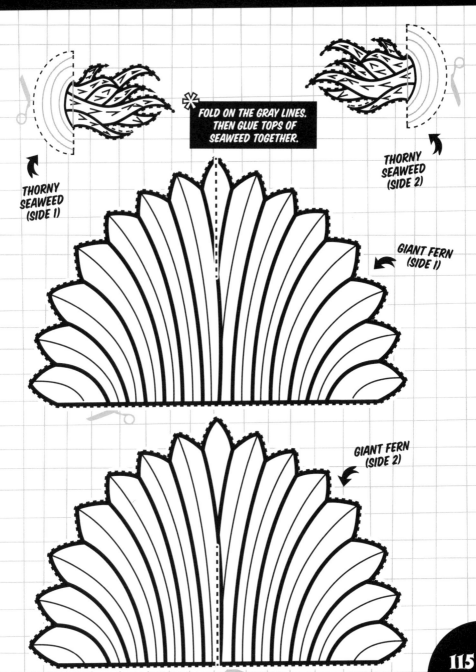

THORNY
SEAWEED
(SIDE 1)

*FOLD ON THE GRAY LINES.
THEN GLUE TOPS OF
SEAWEED TOGETHER.*

THORNY
SEAWEED
(SIDE 2)

GIANT FERN
(SIDE 1)

GIANT FERN
(SIDE 2)

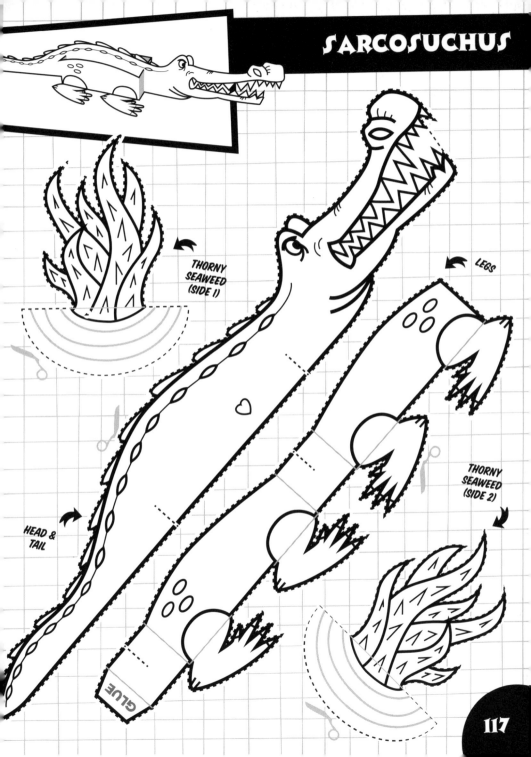

SARCOSUCHUS

THORNY SEAWEED (SIDE 1)

LEGS

THORNY SEAWEED (SIDE 2)

HEAD & TAIL

GLUE

117

SPINOSAURUS (PART 1)

GIANT FLOWER
(SIDE 1)

ARMS

GIANT FLOWER
(SIDE 2)

HEAD &
TAIL

119

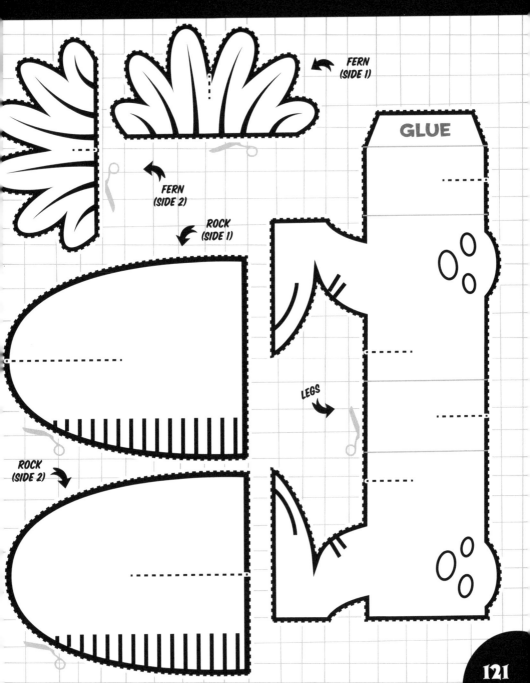

FERN
(SIDE 1)

FERN
(SIDE 2)

ROCK
(SIDE 1)

GLUE

LEGS

ROCK
(SIDE 2)

121

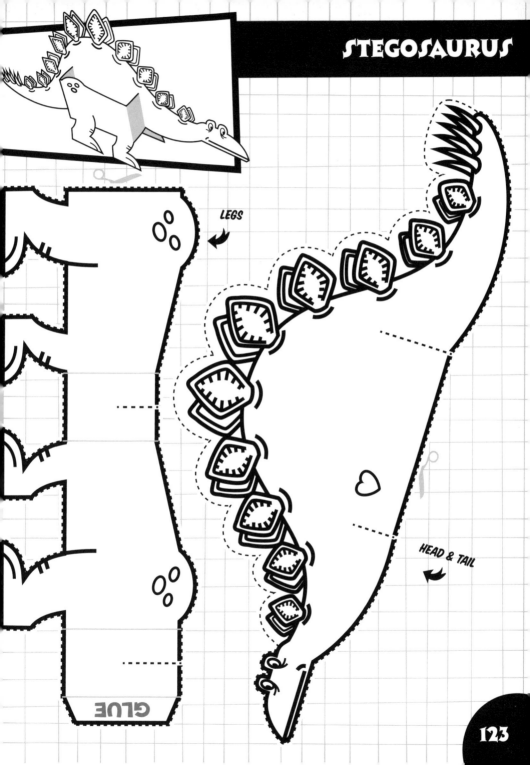

STEGOSAURUS

LEGS

HEAD & TAIL

GLUE

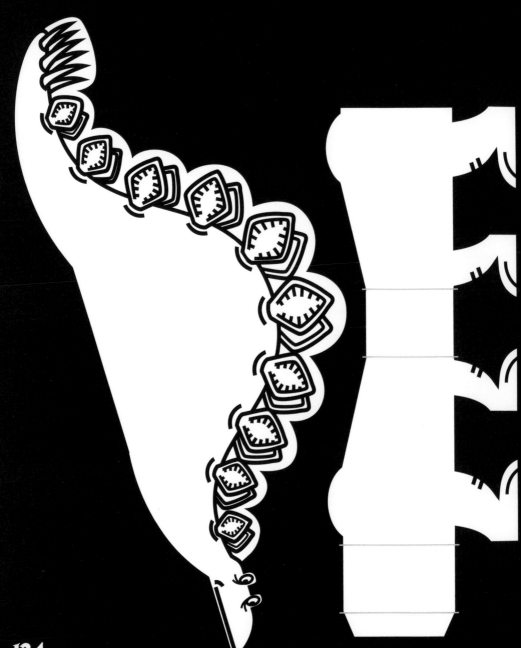

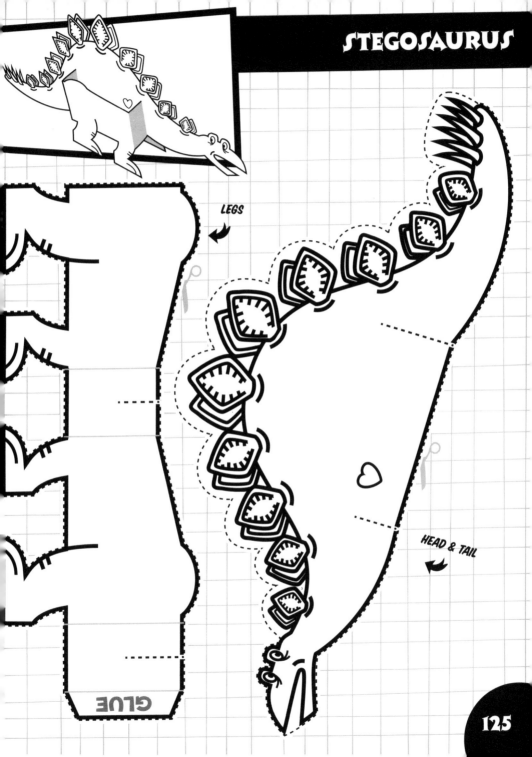

STEGOSAURUS

LEGS

HEAD & TAIL

GLUE

125

STYGIMOLOCH

HORNS

INSERT HORNS HERE

HEAD & TAIL

ARMS

GLUE

LEGS

127

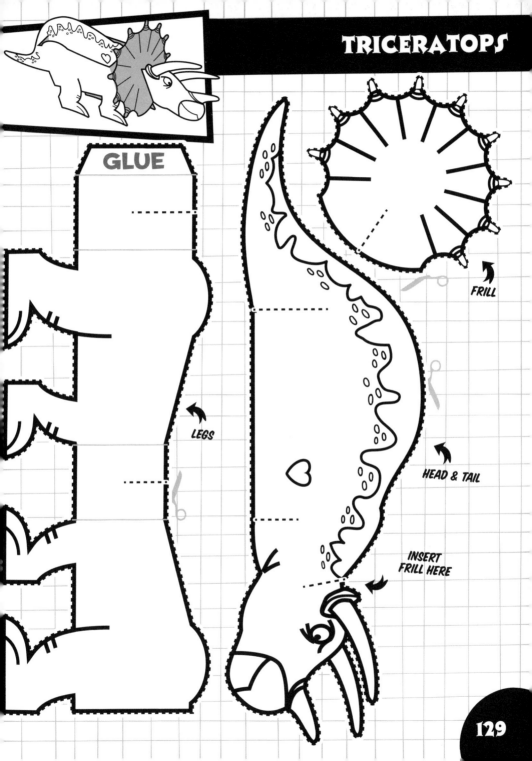

TRICERATOPS

GLUE

FRILL

LEGS

HEAD & TAIL

INSERT FRILL HERE

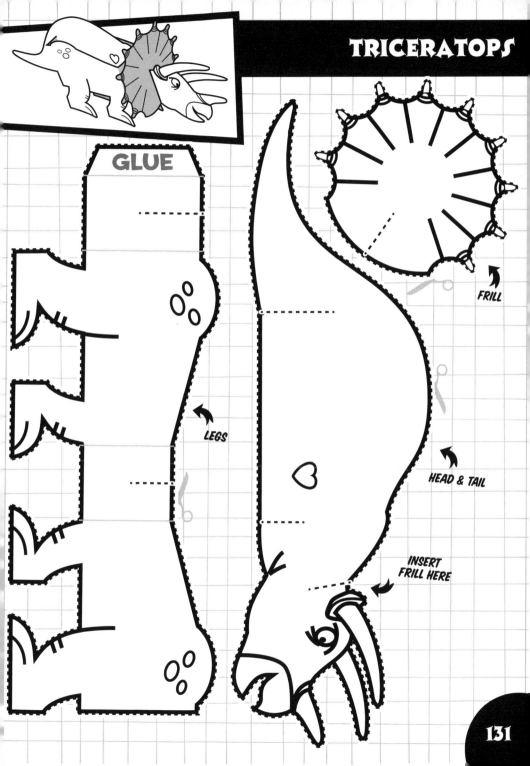

TRICERATOPS

GLUE

FRILL

LEGS

HEAD & TAIL

INSERT FRILL HERE

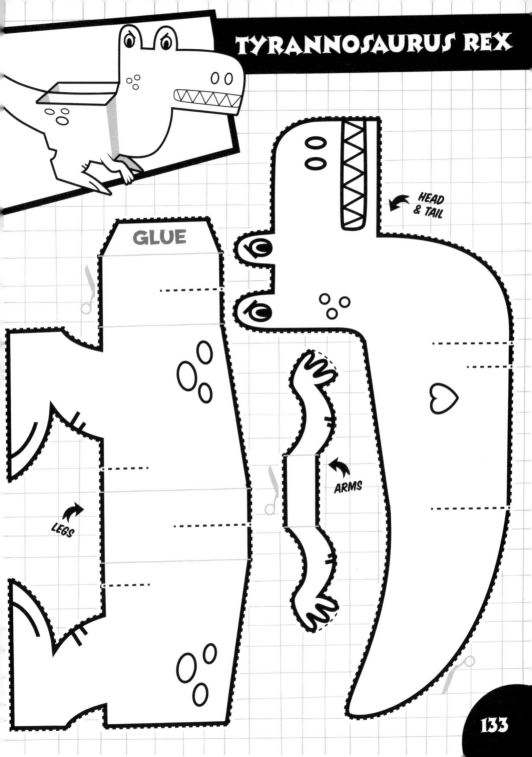

TYRANNOSAURUS REX

GLUE

HEAD & TAIL

ARMS

LEGS

133

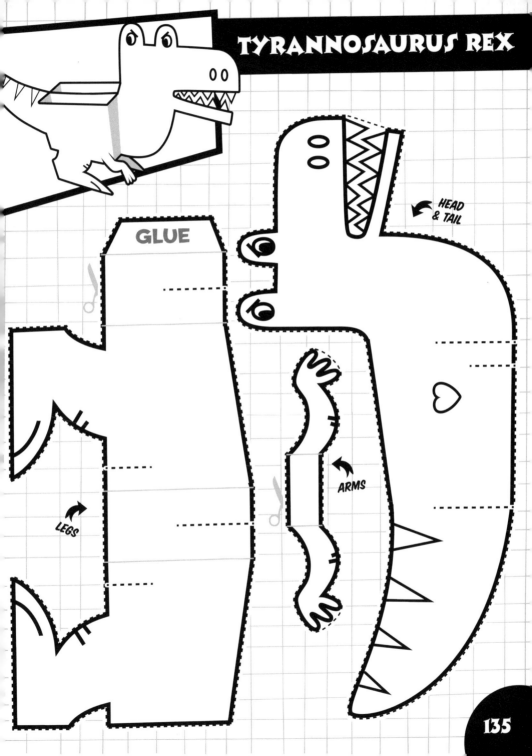

TYRANNOSAURUS REX

HEAD & TAIL

GLUE

LEGS

ARMS

135

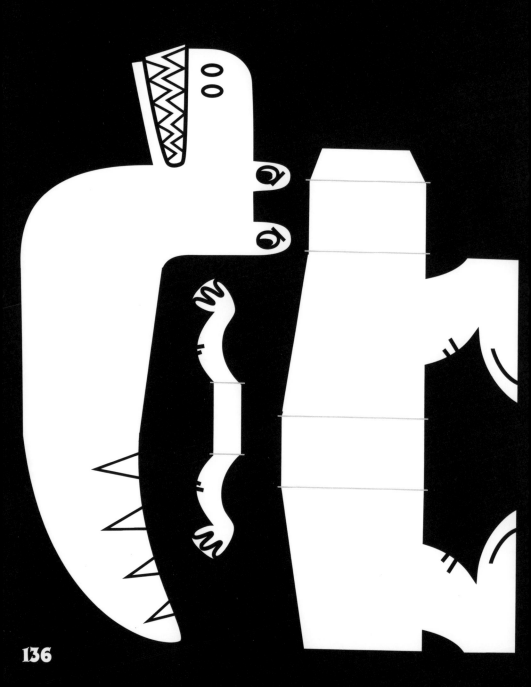

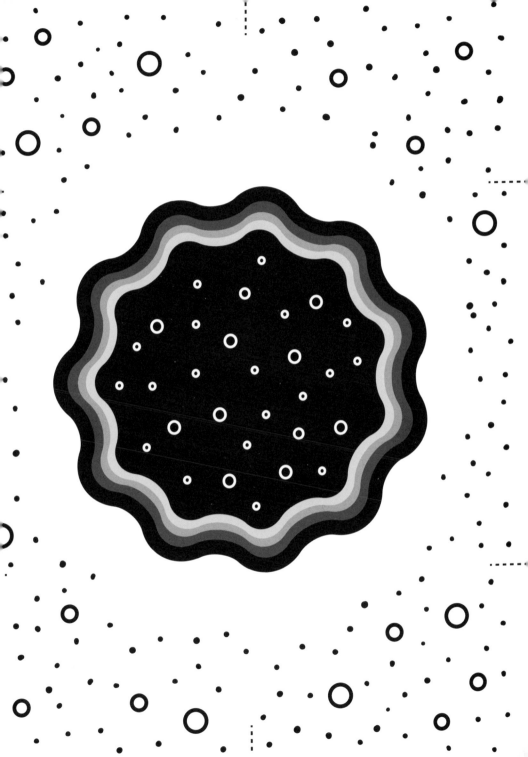

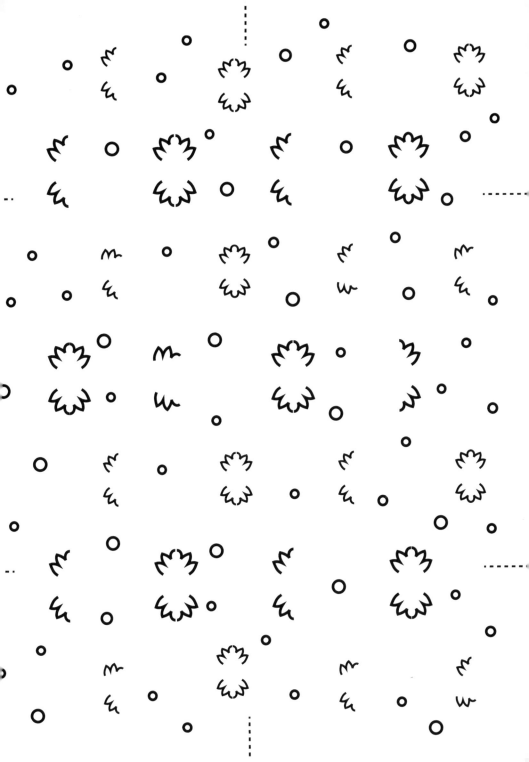

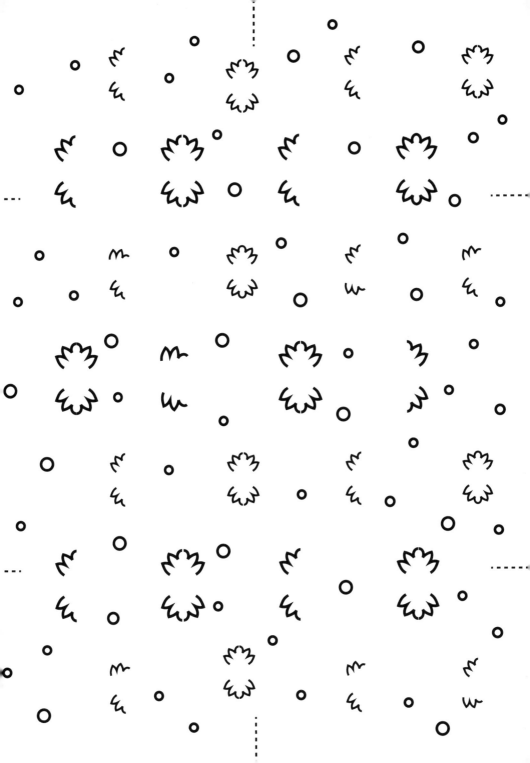

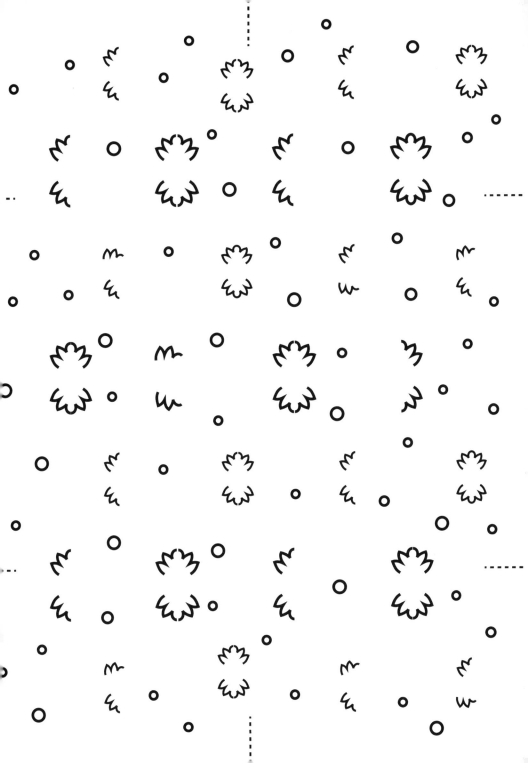

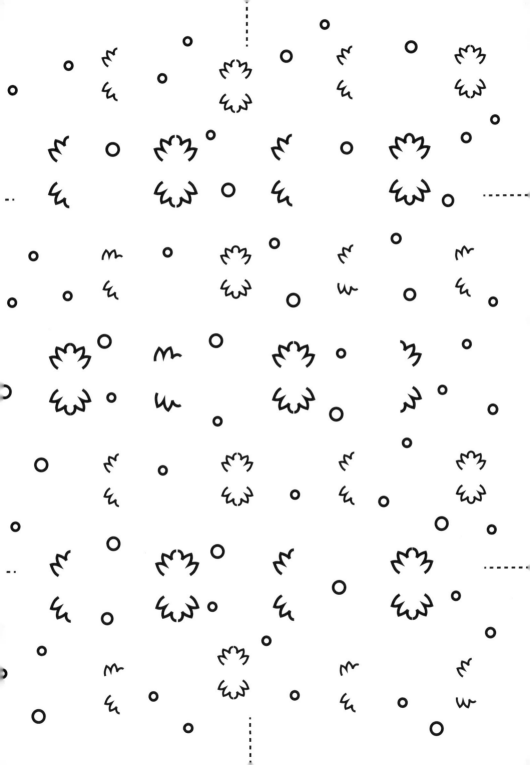

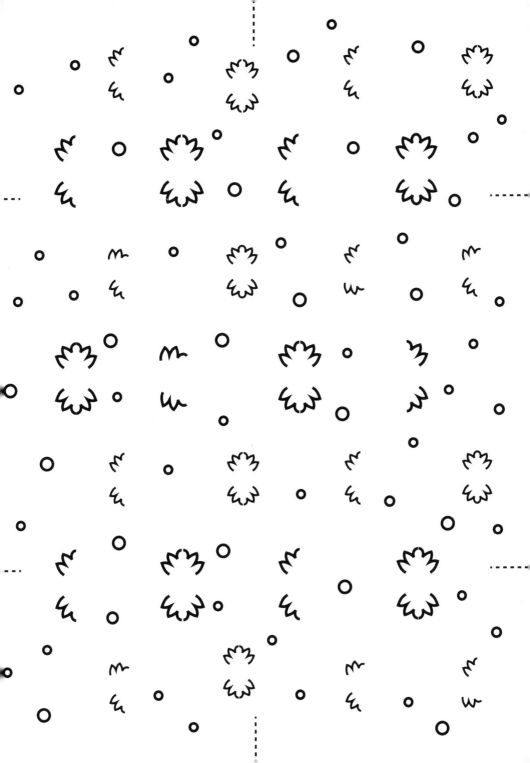

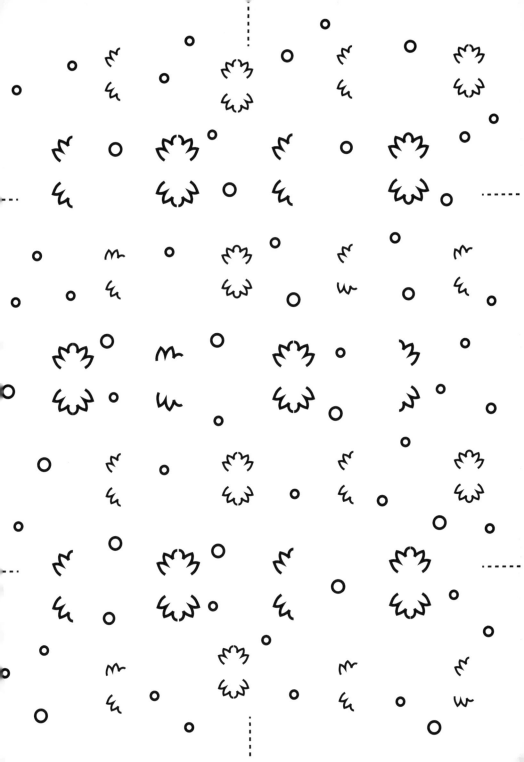

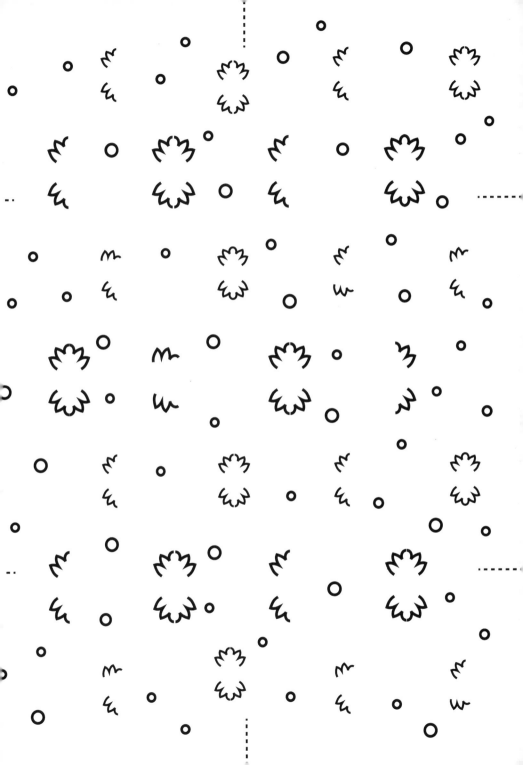